THE LEGEND OF THE KUKUI NUT

story by ROBERT BRANDON HENDERSON
illustrations by MARK McKENNA

ISBN 13: 978-1-59955-119-7

Published by CFI, an imprint of Cedar Fort, Inc.
2373 W. 700 S., Springville, UT 84663
Distributed by Cedar Fort, Inc., www.cedarfort.com

Library of Congress Cataloging-in-Publication Data

Henderson, Brandon (Robert Brandon)
  The legend of the kukui nut / Brandon Henderson.
     p. cm.
  Summary: Journeying in darkness, young Melika burns kukui nuts to illuminate the path and demonstrates her inner light by helping others less fortunate along the way.
  ISBN 978-1-59955-119-7
  [1. Candlenut tree--Folklore. 2. Folklore--Hawaii.] I. Title.

  PZ8.1.H3832Le 2008
  398.2--dc22
  [E]

                    2008008651

Edited by Kimiko Christensen Hammari
Jacket and book design by Nicole Williams
Cover design © 2008 by Lyle Mortimer
Printed on acid-free paper

Printed in Hong Kong
10 9 8 7 6 5 4 3 2 1

DEDICATION

LEGEND

WORD	MEANING
Lani	*Heaven*
Honua	*Earth*
Makua	*God/Father*
Kaula	*Prophet*
Noho ali'i	*Throne*
Aloha	*Love*
Palapala Hemolele	*Scripture/Map*
'Ilihune	*Poor*
Pololi	*Hungry*
Ma'i	*Sick*

Long ago, there was a little girl who lived on the island of Lani. Her name was Melika, and she was very happy.

Every day she wore a kukui nut lei. It was her favorite. Chief Makua had given it to her, along with all of her brothers and sisters, and they loved him very much.

Chief Makua was tall and strong and very kind. He always made time to make leis with the girls and have foot races with the boys.

Every day, Chief Makua would choose one of Melika's brothers or sisters to go to the island of Honua to test their light. It was very dark on Honua, so each time he chose someone, Chief Makua would give that person a bag of kukui nuts, an oil lamp, and a spark to light it, before sending them on their journey.

On a day not very different from any other, Melika and her brothers and sisters gathered together on the top of Mount Noho ali'i to find out who Chief Makua would choose next.

"Melika," he said. "It is your time to go." All at once, Melika felt nervous and excited. "Here is your lamp," said Makua. "Always keep it lit. Never leave it behind." His eyes smiled as he knelt down in front of her and said, "Aloha."

"Aloha," said Melika.

She wrapped her arms around Chief Makua's strong neck and felt his loving arms around her. She closed her eyes and held on tight for what seemed like a long time.

When Melika opened her eyes, Chief Makua was gone. The sun had gone down and she was all alone. "Where is everyone?" she wondered.

Melika called out to see if anyone was there, but no one answered. It was very dark now, and she could hardly see.

"I must be on Honua," thought Melika. "It never gets this dark on Lani. How will I ever get back to Chief Makua and my brothers and sisters when I cannot see?"

Just then, she felt in her hands the oil lamp and the spark that Chief Makua had given to her. She used her spark to try and light the lamp, but it was no use; there was no oil in it.

Melika was so discouraged and scared in that dark place that she began to cry. After a while, she felt so tired from being sad and afraid that she fell asleep.

When she awoke, she saw a light through the trees and thought it might be the sun rising.

"What is your name?" asked the light. Melika was so astonished that the sun was speaking to her that she rubbed her eyes, thinking it was a dream.

When she looked again, she saw that the light was not coming from the sun but from an oil lamp, just like hers. A small man with glad eyes stood in front of her, holding the lamp.

"You do have a name, don't you?" asked the man.

"Yes . . . of course . . . Melika is my name," she responded.

"My name is Kaula, and it is a pleasure to meet you."

Not knowing what else to say, Melika asked Kaula, "Do you know how to get back to Chief Makua and my family?"

"I was hoping you were going to ask me that. Follow me," said Kaula with his glad eyes and a large smile.

As Melika followed Kaula, light began to grow around her. After passing through a large patch of ferns and bushes, they entered a clearing filled with people. Each person held a lamp like Melika's, although not all were as bright as Kaula's.

Many people had the same bag of kukui nuts that Melika had, but some were not as full as hers. "They must have lost them," thought Melika.

Melika looked at Kaula's bag and noticed it was almost empty. Only one kukui nut remained.

After passing through the crowd, Melika and Kaula came to a small hut at the center of the clearing. "After you," said Kaula to Melika, motioning for her to enter.

"Have a seat," said Kaula. "I have something special to show you."

Kaula walked to a tall stack of rolled papers, took one off the top, and handed it to Melika. "This is called the Palapala Hemolele," said Kaula. "It will guide you home."

Melika opened the paper to see a simple map guiding her path back to the island of Lani and Chief Makua. "Oh, thank you, Kaula," said Melika. "But how will I see my way in the dark having no oil for my lamp?"

"I will show you," said Kaula, and he reached into his almost empty bag and pulled out his last kukui nut.

"May I?" he asked as he reached for her bag of nuts.

"Of course," said Melika.

Kaula took a kukui nut from Melika's bag and with his nut, cracked open Melika's. Oil splashed out of both Melika's and Kaula's kukui nuts as they struck one another.

Carefully Kaula poured the oil from his kukui nut into his own lamp and then poured the oil from Melika's kukui nut into hers.

"Use your spark," he said, and Melika's lamp immediately burst into flame, mixing with Kaula's light to add to the brightness of the room.

"It is wonderful," said Melika. "Mahalo."

"Mahalo," said Kaula.

"Now, before you go, remember to never leave your lamp behind and to always keep it lit," said Kaula.

"But what if I run out of oil?" asked Melika.

"Follow the map, and you will always have oil in your lamp," said Kaula.

"Aloha, safe journey," said Kaula as he waved good-bye to Melika.

"Aloha," said Melika.

As Melika followed the map, she heard something that sounded like a boy crying. "Hello?" she called out. "Is anybody there?"

"Help!" cried a voice. "I am stuck!"

Melika quickly followed the sound to a small beach next to the ocean. She found a young boy, not much older than her, sitting in the sand with his foot caught between two large stones.

"How did you get here? Are you okay?" asked Melika.

"I was playing too close to the water and got stuck between these two stones," said the boy. "Can you help me?" asked the boy.

"I can try," said Melika.

Melika looked around to see what she could use to help the boy, but nothing seemed like a good idea. Not knowing what else to do, Melika took one of the kukui nuts from her bag and cracked it open on one of the rocks. Oil spilled everywhere, including on the boy's foot.

"I am able to move my foot!" said the boy, and soon his foot was free. "Mahalo," he said. "You saved me."

"Mahalo," said Melika.

At that moment, Melika's lamp burned brighter than ever before. Both Melika and the boy were astonished.

"Do you know how to get back to Chief Makua?" asked the boy. "I was hoping you were going to ask me that," responded Melika with a smile.

"My name is Melika," she said. "What is yours?"

"Palanakonu," said the boy. "It is nice to meet you."

From then on, Melika and Palanakonu journeyed together to find their way back to Chief Makua. While on their journey, they met and helped many people.

For many days, they followed the map along beautiful white sand beaches. However, as time went on, the beaches became very rocky.

Eventually all the sand was gone, and the shores were covered in large black stones. The stones were sharp and very dangerous.

While they traveled along this rocky terrain, it began to rain. The stones became very slippery and hard to walk on. Melika lost her balance and scraped her elbow on one of the stones while trying to protect her lamp from shattering. "That was close," she said as she rubbed her now stinging elbow.

"We better get out of the rain," said Palanakonu. "The light in your lamp is beginning to dim."

Melika and Palanakonu searched for shelter. They found a small cave in one of the rocks and crawled inside.

As they entered the cave, they were startled by a voice in the darkness, and they shined their lamps in its direction.

"Welcome," said the voice. It belonged to a very elderly-looking man who was wearing little more than rags for clothes.

"The light you carry is very warm," said the man. "Would you share some of it with me?"

"Of course," said Melika and Palanakonu. Immediately, Palanakonu searched the cave to find a few dry pieces of wood to start a fire, while Melika unfolded a small blanket which she had and wrapped it around the old man's shoulders.

"My name is 'Ilihune," said the old man. "Mine is Melika, and this is Palanakonu," said Melika.

"Mahalo," said the man.

"Mahalo," they responded.

After spending a few days with 'Ilihune, Melika and Palanakonu continued on their journey. After many days, they came to a large city.

The city had large buildings and enormous pyramids with many steps on every side. They were astonished by how many people lived in the city.

Many of the women in the city wore very fine dresses and had beautiful jewelry. Melika imagined how wonderful it would be for her to have such nice things. She saw a young woman trading a few kukui nuts for a set of golden earrings in a small shop and thought, "Maybe I can trade just a few."

As she began to walk toward the shop, Melika felt a light tug on the back of her skirt. She turned around to meet a pair of large brown eyes, which belonged to a small girl.

The girl was younger than Melika and looked very thin. "Will you help us?" asked the girl in a quiet but very concerned voice. "My brother is sick, and we don't have any money to buy him the medicine he needs."

Tears were welling up in the girl's eyes, but before they could fall, Palanakonu took one of her hands and said, "Yes, we will help you."

At first, Melika felt disappointed, but as the girl's sadness turned to hope and she smiled the biggest smile Melika had ever seen, she knew that this was much more important than pretty jewelry.

The little girl pulled Melika by the hand down a side street, and Palanakonu followed close behind.

"What is your name?" asked Melika as they ran through the city. "Pololi," said the girl. "We're almost there."

Soon they arrived at the door of a small hut, just on the outskirts of the city.

When they entered, the darkness thickened and Melika held her lamp higher.

A small straw bed sat in the corner of the room. Lying on it was a boy. He was smaller and younger than Pololi. Even in the dark, Melika could tell he was very pale.

Melika sat on the edge of the bed and placed her hand on the young boy's arm and said, "Hello, my name is Melika and this is my friend Palanakonu. We are here to help you."

The boy's eyes opened weakly, and a faint smile crossed his lips. "His name is Ma'i," said Pololi.

For many weeks, Melika and Palanakonu took care of Pololi and Ma'i, using their kukui nuts to light fires and trade for food and medicine. Day by day the darkness in the little hut faded as the brightness of their lamps grew.

After Ma'i recovered, Melika and Palanakonu said good-bye to him and Pololi and continued on their journey to find Chief Makua.

Throughout their travels they met many more people. Each time they used their kukui nuts to help someone, their lamps grew brighter, until one day when Melika realized that she had no kukui nuts left. Melika and Palanakonu were near the end of their journey, and although they had no oil left to put in their lamps, the light coming from them was as bright as ever.

As they climbed a large mountain, a thick white fog gathered around them and they got separated from each other. "Melika!" cried Palanakonu.

"Palanakonu!" cried Melika. But neither heard a response.

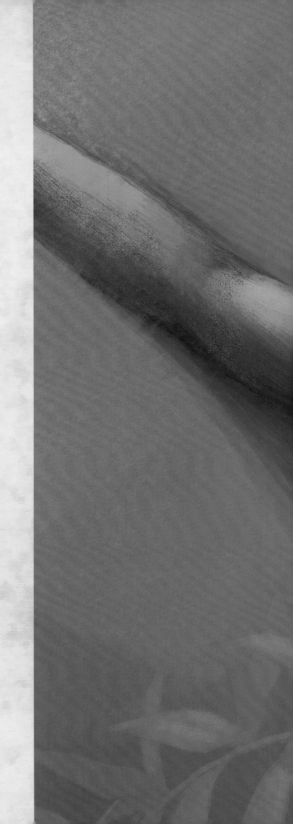

Although Melika was alone and sad that she had lost her friend, she continued to follow the map leading to Chief Makua. The mountain soon became very steep and it was difficult to climb, especially while holding her lamp. Melika was getting very tired as she came to a steep cliff. The fog was now so thick that she couldn't see the top. Her lamp felt heavy in her hand, and she thought of leaving it behind. But she remembered the words of Kaula: "Never leave your lamp behind and always keep it lit." With determination, Melika began to climb. Her heart felt warmed by the lamp in her hand, and she fought with all her might. Melika's arms and legs grew weak as she neared the top. She could see the fog clearing just a few feet above her. Melika reached with all of her strength, still holding tight to her lamp, but as she stretched, her foot slipped and she felt herself begin to fall. At that moment, she felt a large, strong hand grip her wrist and begin to pull her up.

"Hello, Melika," said a familiar voice.

Slowly, Melika looked up and stared into a large pair of smiling eyes. "Chief Makua!" cried Melika. "I finally found you!" "You never lost me," said Chief Makua, and he pointed downward.

"The island of Honua!" said Melika in surprise. "But what are you doing here?" she asked. Then Chief Makua pointed upward.

"The island of Lani!" she exclaimed, realizing that Lani and Honua were the same place—you just had to be standing in the right place to see it.

"Melika!" cried another familiar voice.

"Palanakonu!" cried Melika as she and her friend hugged.

"I have a gift for you two," said Chief Makua, and he gave each of them a kukui nut lei. "These represent the light you gave to others and the light you kept in your hearts."

Taking each by the hand, Chief Makua led Melika and Palanakonu up Mount Noho ali'i. "Aloha," he said.

And with tears in their eyes, they responded, "Aloha."

THE END

11/29/09